The characters and events portrayed in this book are fictitious. Any similarity to real persons, living or dead, is coincidental and not intended by the authors.

The e-book version of this book is intended as a free sample in the form of a Prelude to "Timeless' Aria: The Sapphire Shore". It may not be sold, edited, or repurposed, or reproduced, or redistributed outside of its official distribution points.

This printed version has been priced to cover its printing costs and is being made available for those that prefer a physical medium.

ISBN (Paperback): 978-3-911111-01-0
ISBN (Hardcover): 978-3-911111-03-4

Reports of Rebellion

12th OF FIRST SPRING 496 F.O.

FOR THE EYES OF THE SCRYING MANTIS

Five documents I have prepared for your deliberation.

These contain our full recount of the most recent Rigatan attempt at secession. This follows the previous rebellion attempt ended by High Warmaster **Ragos** twenty-one years, two seasons and three days prior. I have launched an inquiry with the prominent trusted figures that helped quell this act of treason. They have all been cooperative, leaving out no detail that I could discern and faithfully recounting their actions and thoughts.

I have compiled the results of my inquiry in the shape of a full account of the proceedings. I have also carefully transcribed the dates and locations for completeness.

I have made an attempt at brevity as well, following instructions of haste given by the Arch Mantis. Our attention must swiftly turn to the hornet nest, before they find amidst themselves a repugnant queen. As improbable a thought as that might seem.

Scurrying Mantis

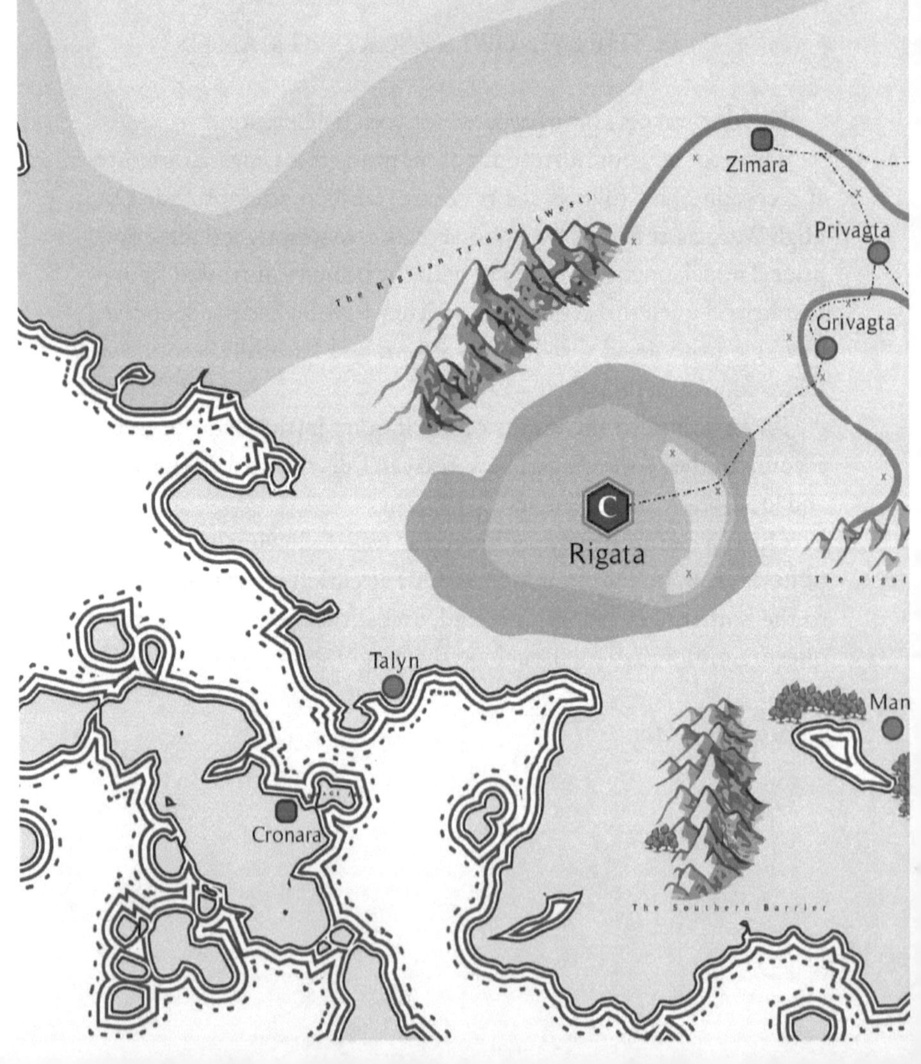

Map of Rigata
(And neighbouring realms)
The Opulent Desert
Zimara
Privagta
Grivagta
The Rigatan Trident (West)
Rigata
The Rigat
Talyn
Man
Cronara
The Southern Barrier

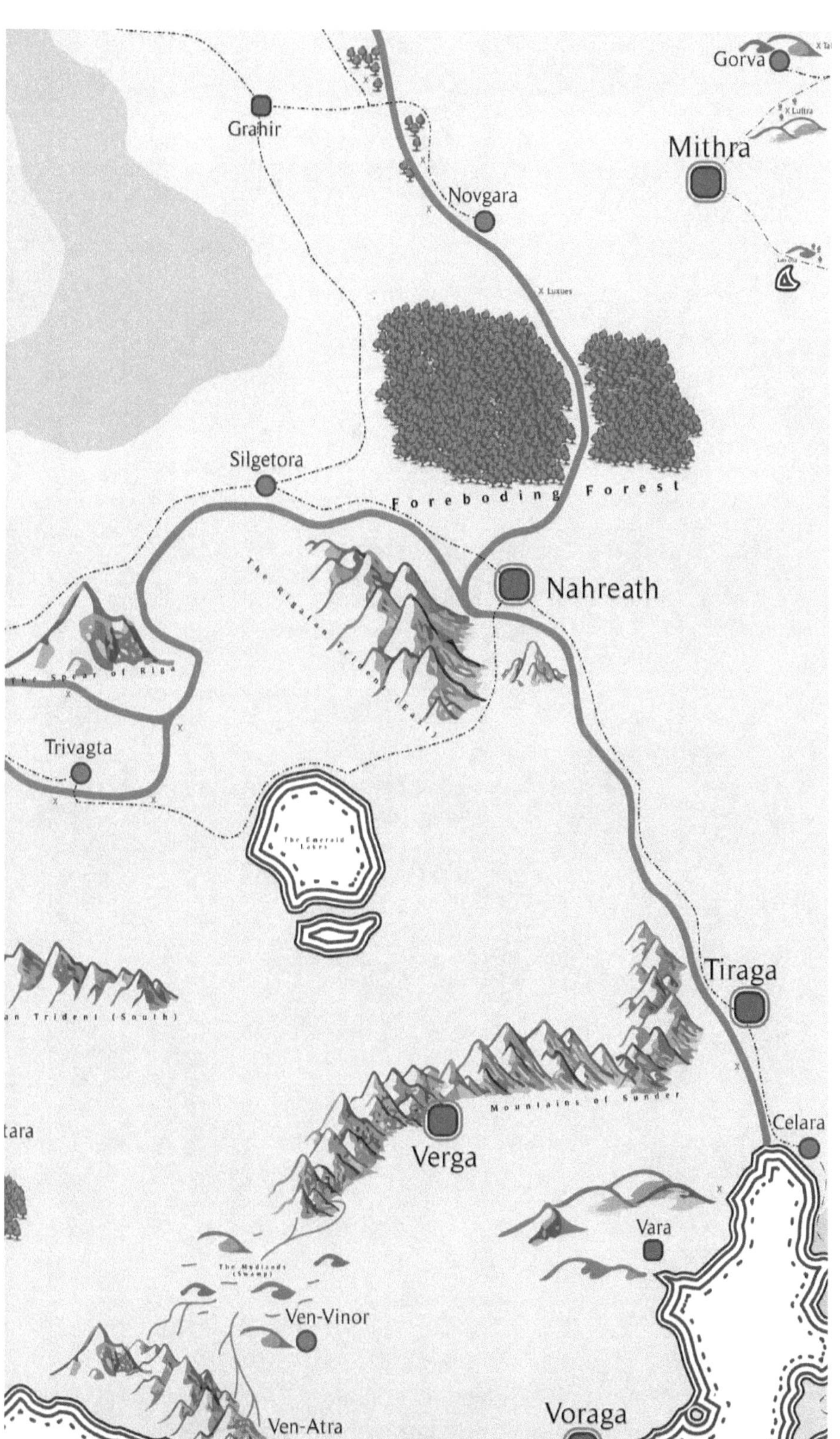

Gorva
Mithra
X Luftra
Grahir
Novgara
X Luxues
Foreboding Forest
Silgetora
Nahreath
The Spear of Riga
Trivagta
The Emerald Isles
Tiraga
an Trident (South)
Mountains of Sunder
Celara
Verga
Vara
tara
The Mudlands
(Swamp)
Ven-Vinor
Voraga
Ven-Atra

Spark

27th OF SECOND SPRING 495 F.O.

"From spark a fire in hearth was born
And shone upon a couple now torn
A man with duty and oath once sworn
A woman of beauty yet heart well worn"

After the first spoken stanza, a flurry of clapping and drumming filled the air, signalling the start of the energetic Rigatan jingle. Soon, a melody sparked and music joined in.

"How steep, the cost for sleep once fought?
How deep, your love for me once caught?
What pride, you carry for Rigata ought?
What fills and lives in your every thought?

She asked near smoke with eye bearing tear
Reflected agleam and grimly in his gear

I rest only when my enemies fall
Banners raised high I'll slay them all
To you I'll return so proud and tall
For I must answer nation's call

He said as the flame lit his eyes ablaze
Little did he care for worry to erase

I fear the screams of our dying youth

Spark

I fear in your eyes delusions of truth
I hear the echo of a gravestone smooth
I hear my heart screaming 'nothing would soothe'

Unease as the fire cackled with no end
The fear that his life be needlessly spent

I fight for our king and for you my dear
I fight for your smile from ear to ear
To you I'll return with boisterous cheer
To you in a year, so erase all fear

He doused the fire and turned to dash
He left his lover to reckon with ash

O road be steady and carry his feet
O fields show mercy should a foe he meet
O sun be warm abstain your heat
O fortune smile and spare defeat

She sighed in a haze as she watched from the door
Her lover depart, whom she saw no more

For his was to end their greatest of wars
Hers was to wallow in the quarrel of the stars"

This was her song, composed and delivered in Rigata's heightened tempo. Though laced with enough of her signature high pitched voice to make out of herself an object of their fancy more so than the song itself.

Beyond lies a detailed record of her initial venture regarding a possible Rigatan rebellion. I, who shall remain unnamed, speak on behalf of our **Orchid Mantis** of bardic fame, then serving as our informant stationed in the Rigatan city of Trivagta.

This is a recount of what came of her endeavour in the south.

***

.

"Bravo, my lady bard, Bravo." It was one of their prominent captains that approached her first after her song. He was a man that seemed to have seen more battle with parchment than with sword, at least as far as a first glance betrayed. His armour was ornate, fit for the occasion, though he barely filled it. His hair was long and marvellously unwearied by war, as was his thin, kempt face and un-intimidating demeanour.

"I am pleased to entertain." She bowed her head and ever so slightly bent at one knee while grabbing at the sides of her dress. There was no doubt in her mind that her performance indeed entertained him. Though she suspected that what he saw in her did not go past her hazel gems of eyes, long, full dark hair, or apparent elegance and, in his own words, 'beauty'.

"Entertain? You, my lady, inspire." He said, and again she did not doubt his words in the slightest. "Like no other you do, in fact, it would honour me to have you dine along with my company. You have set the tone masterfully for this night, and I would have you share in the ambience you helped set."

"I am flattered to warrant a seat at so noble a table."

"I'm afraid, my lady, that no table in Rigata does you justice."

Orchid had worked long and hard to get to that point.

To find herself in that particular hall, with these men gathered.

'Even now, my task has merely begun.'

Until this point, Orchid had only mentioned in her previous accounts and reports that the dissonance in Rigata to Hydarian rule was merely the talk of common folk. Words of those who had no means to incite action, or entice change.

"Shall we?" He presented a hand, and she gracefully took it. The thin captain walked her over slowly to the wide wooden table in question, and there she could see them. Prince **Renedil**'s table, in whose name this banquet was thrown, was two tables away from her escort's own table full of captains and other prominent figures of the Rigatan army.

'And here I thought these were times of peace.'

"I must say, your song was particularly touching to me." He admitted, and she painfully realised how slowly he was deliberately walking.

*'He truly does honour his brother's memory. The valiant man that he was, a warrior of such renown, that he was sent atop his company to break the Sapphire Gates of **Mithra**. Only back then they were no more than hastily cobbled battlements. Had I not happened upon his story, I doubt I could have composed a song of such efficacy.'*

She gave him a quaint nod and a pleased smile that hid her layered thoughts. Then she stole another gaze at Prince Renedil's table, and immediately she noticed them.

'Renedil's guard? Out in force too, suspicious show of force for such a simple banquet.'

There would be no chance to study them, for Orchid soon engaged in what she called 'dangerous drivel'. She was now dining with these captains, and was being asked about many things that ought to be entirely menial. Though should she handle these questions oddly, she risked drawing suspicion to herself. During this drivel, she poised herself to remain wary of Renedil's entourage, especially one guard that stood out.

'Even for Renedil's own guard, that one is better built, more muscular, and far too alert for the occasion. His hand hovers ever so dearly near his needlessly large spear. Never have I seen a Rigatan with such striking green eyes, like emeralds captured within his gaze. Is he a mere guard, or perhaps a Royal Guard? And of course, my eyes have betrayed me. I've stolen a glance too many.'

"Listen to reason," a man from her table spoke, bringing her attention back to the ongoing conversation. "Hydaria is mightier than ever, and its rule has been kind. They have bolstered our trade through the Riverlands to their capital in the north and have protected our interests and lands against Migora. I see no reason in giving more credence to the unweighed words of common folk whose hearts are so easily swayed."

"You say that Hydaria has protected our interests?" Orchid's Captain raised his voice, then clenched his first to contain himself. "Is that what they were doing when they had us break against those wretched Sapphire Gates? They fed us to Mithra's flames readily and retreated when we were spent! They are no more than decadent cowards whose worthier ancestors have uplifted to a position of unstable strength. Witless in war and exploitative in rule. There is naught to the wisdom of their Emperor and the tact of their High Warmaster but lies and propaganda."

"I for one agree," another voice added, and Orchid noted the rank and station of those that were now openly questioning Hydaria's sovereignty. Even now she worked associations in her mind and awaiting the names to marry with their faces. "You also say they are mightier than ever, but it was not too long ago that Ragos, their fool of a High Warmaster, led his storied army into Migora. Only to be bit back by the same flame that guards the east. Mithra tossed him out reeling into the desert, scattering his mind along with his armies, and some say he has not been the same since returning to power. He is most certainly not the same Ragos that denied us our freedom all those years past."

"And the will of the common folk is not a trifling matter. We are not Hydarians, where the common folk are naught more than sacks of tax in the eyes of the nobility." Another agreed, and Orchid's list grew to make room for those that were potentially a concern. Though quickly she realised how futile a task it was, and how much easier it was to count those that remained loyal.

"It warms my heart to see that my lords take the opinion of lesser men so highly." Orchid said, bringing about a healthy variety of smug expressions along with pleased faces. "Though I fear I have been too engrossed in my work to take leave of it. Once, I sang of naught but the strife of our people, but I fear I have grown ill informed. Tell me, my good lords, how badly does our realm ail?"

"Allow me to shed light on the matter then," the thin captain said. "My lady, I am well connected here in Trivagta. I have been in recent contact with multiple farmsteads, and the reports grow grimmer by the day. Most of all report angst, with Hydaria's sudden need for grain of late, along with the frankly obscene capacity of the Hydarian army, they are left with naught to fend for themselves. Not after covering the fee for transporting goods to their vile Hydarian capital in the far north!"

"All the way to Orvabad from here?" She mused, with a trained, pleasant look on her face.

"Yes! Which naturally leaves our own cities underfed," another man added, who seemed to be far more invested in this matter than Orchid's Captain. "And it ties up our transport network, and it leaves us at the mercy of the rain, all in service of the Hydarian army's belly."

"Ragos is mustering an army to end the war, is what they said."

"And should he win that war, Rigata will truly come under the sword."

"When our merchants and farmers grow poor, so will the land."

The further this conversation dragged on, the more people turned to their food and drink in silence, hoping to avoid such a thorny topic. Though there was a discerning lack of any enthusiasm for the spread of food on offer, despite how aromatic and mouth watering it otherwise would have been.

The tedious dinner conversation was only broken by one man who dared to defend Hydarian rule, but even he grew tired of the never-ending chatter of how the sun would shine brighter without Hydarians leading Rigata. In a brief fit of anger, and at one comment Orchid failed to note, he excused himself from the table and left the banquet.

It was then that Orchid saw two guards from Renedil's company pursue him out.

"A fool." One said grimly, as the mood over their table turned sourer than the lime left floating in his liquor. "Knows not what to say, or when. He would rather buzz as annoyingly as a fly, only to be smitten down by ruling hands."

'I thought I made no errors.'

Orchid knew herself to be a capable informant, but that statement threw her off guard. Suddenly she wondered if she had been invited to this table of her own design, or if she had been lured into it.

"Forgive the foul mood, my lady. Care to join me for some fresh air?" The captain that fancied her said, and Orchid felt a chill run down her spine.

'I have no choice.'

"How thoughtful of you. It would be my pleasure." She calmly stood and let the man walk her away from the table.

Then she heard Prince Renedil stand and address his gathered audience.

'I have to report this.'

"We'll miss the prince's speech-" Orchid started, but felt the man's grip on her arm tighten as he led her to the balcony.

'He knows too? How? I took every precaution.'

"I'm afraid, my lady, that the prince will impart military information."

"Forgive me, I did not know."

She smiled with a lowered head.

They finally emerged into the open air of the balcony, and the man let her go. Then the man turned slowly, and she took a further step towards the open terrace. She heard the doors to the balcony close and a key turn to lock, and through it all she stood steadfast, gazing towards the horizon and holding her breath.

The young captain walked past her, much to her surprise. There, he clasped the rails with both hands and the wind blew through his long hair.

'Suspicion or vanity? Which is it?'

"There is nothing to forgive," he said and watched the fields extend beyond Trivagta's walls. Then an all too familiar sound creaked, and Orchid could feel her heart thump in her chest.

The chirping and clicking of grasshoppers.

The man didn't turn to her. He stood there gazing into the distance, and as she remained behind him for a vacant moment, resisting the urge to turn, she heard him sigh.

"Besides, I would very much rather hear that song again, to the backdrop of Rigatan fields, and with that pleasant hum in the ambience."

Orchid felt her throat dry as she was being asked to sing to the tune of grasshoppers when she was sent to scry upon them. With complete uncertainty in the man's intentions, she decided she would remain the bard she was pretending to be for as long as she needed to. Even though that would mean her first reports of a restive Rigata came late.

'Sing I shall then, and sing I shall.'

UPHEAVALS IN THE NORTH

FOR THE EYES OF THE SCRYING MANTIS

Murmurings in the north continue to unsettle the owners of farmlands across the far reaches of the **Euclad** River.

The constant resurgence of northern tremors troubles the more simple-minded folk. Leading to many tall tales about *'Worms of the North'*, *'Monsters of the Lake'*, and *'Tunnellers in the Dark'*. A troubled populace is ineffective, and not only that, but they have proven to be dishonest as well. These tales have sown enough discord among the farmhands to incite them into stealing livestock, burning the land around where it had been, and claiming this is the work of a monstrosity.

The town most affected by this recent wave of unyielding fictitious tales is the town of **Tancha**. And while the yield of crops and produce from these far northern reaches is of lower quality, lesser quantity, and worth only kibble in any normal circumstance. I am afraid that even these supplies are of great import, given the recent mustering commanded by our Lord Ragos.

A small disciplinary force was sent north, and very much unsurprisingly, reports of tremors have since stopped altogether. With no evidence to suggest this as a mere coincidence.

Winter Mantis

Smoke

26th OF FIRST SUMMER 496 F.O.

Armsmaster **Lysiac**'s company had many strange encounters before they reached their destination. The city of Trivagta, deep in the heart of the Rigatan lands. It was a long and harsh journey, yet it seems like the **Dragon Mantis** had elected to retell it out of order, if only to force it to make sense in his own mind. He left a patient and precise man only to return burdened by his travels and wearied by his thoughts. What follows is a compilation of summaries and reordering of his recounts of the events that transpired.

*****

It seems as if the urgency of Orchid's report was not made as apparent in her initial report as she had hoped. The task to travel to Rigatan lands and investigate such rumours of rebellious intents was left lingering within Hydarian lands for far too long. Until by some act of chance, news found its way to the offices of the newly graduated Armsmaster Lysiac, whose enthusiasm to undertake the task was riveting. The young Armsmaster chose promising yet freshly recruited apprentices to join his company, along with a few trusted men.

Lysiac's company travelled light, yet slower than they ought to have. The Armsmaster seemed to be an admirer of all manner of blades, daggers, sabres, cutlasses, rapiers and broadswords. He insisted upon many stops to smithies and merchants of peculiar weapons, further slowing their pace. The company travelled leisurely throughout the spring and into summer, past the northern

Riverlands and to the far outskirts of Rigata. During their stay in the Riverlands, Lysiac beckoned his Quartermasters and a fellow Armsmaster to gather by the naked city of Silgetora, their last station.

Once inside Rigatan lands, discretion proved to be no great challenge. The Dragon Mantis aside, their company comprised of one Quartermaster, three Tentmasters presiding over a dozen new apprentices each, and a few young mantises hidden amidst these recruits. A sizeable group, but not an overly suspicious presence, not with their leader masquerading as a weapons collector.

At the Rigatan city of **Zimara**, they rested for a week. The Dragon Mantis was quick to collect reports and intelligence. This being the first real chance presented for him to showcase his mettle and flourish in his element. Firstly, he conducted himself as an official envoy from Hydaria and took to questioning the city's local Rigatan officials. Later, as a proficient mantis, he extended his hand to the Hydarian infesting spies and found knowledge aplenty falling to his palms. Yet it was not the quantity of details that alarmed him, but its quality, or rather, lack thereof.

'We had originally set out tasked with dispelling concerns and responding to otherwise ignorable reports of civil unrest within Rigata.' The Dragon Mantis noted. *'I heard the young Armsmaster was waiting for a chance to march with some of his more promising recruits, so his apparent lack of interest in the mission at hand does not surprise me. What does surprise me is the complete lack of worry or otherwise evidence of unrest, let alone a rebellion, that comes from these locals. Not one angry merchant nor rash captain openly discussing his feelings about their sovereign, albeit officially sister, nation of Hydaria? Preposterous! As a spy, I refuse to believe it. If that is by the design of these Rigatan lords, then they vastly overplayed their hand.'*

Armsmaster Lysiac quickly agreed.

He assumed and concluded that the spy network had either been compromised or otherwise lay under enough surveillance to restrict their movements.

The Dragon Mantis set about more tried and trusted ways of gathering information; the hearsay and rumours of the townsfolk.

His mantises spread like wildfire and showed results before long, leaving him to read and reflect deep into the night by candlelight, as he was wont to do.

'Two patterns presented themselves to me, emerging from the groupings of my speculations. The first regarded bandits and common thieves who've taken to blocking trade routes. Their plots served not only to disturb merchants, but also messages from the Rigatan mainland towards the northern borders. The second consideration concerned soldiers and captains returning home abruptly. Many of which discharged from the service of their Landmasters, and by extension the Rigatan army, without proper cause or justification. I took my summary to Armsmaster Lysiac and his eyes lit up. Commands were barked, and we marched south. Yet, I was also tasked with sending an urgent report to the Riverlands with a swift rider asking for reinforcements to be made ready.'

The company moved further south-east for a few days before they happened upon the Spear of Riga, a treacherous mountain range to the east of the path to Trivagta. After a further five days of more inspired marching than their original pacing, their view changed. The imposing mountains of The Spear loomed far in the distance as they passed by them, painted in shades of green and white. Armsmaster Lysiac veered their company towards it and soon reached the soaring mountain's foot.

Before the waning golden lights of the day faded, they stood admiring the stupendous mountain in awe. Suddenly, an echo disturbed their stupor, forcing life onto their company.

Loud, full of malice.

Battle cries echoed.

Men descended upon their company like angry waves from a steep waterfall, yet they fell upon stubborn and unwavering rocks.

Armsmaster Lysiac led the vanguard into a makeshift formation, three columns of apprentices and soldiers, each led by their respective Tentmaster.

At their centre stood Quartermaster **Kiganac**, a large and fierce fighter who showed his mettle on that brief night. The Quartermaster was quick to anger and grunted heavily as he lopped off heads indiscriminately. Armsmaster Lysiac, however, was strangely methodical and reserved in his fighting. He injured and incapacitated most of the men unlucky enough to cross his blade.

The entire ordeal lasted for a few brief moments before the rest of the assailants realised; they were outmatched and soon to be outnumbered. The remnants of these criminals slipped into the foot of the mountain under the veil of darkness. Like poured wine escaping into the cracks of a poorly assembled terrace.

In the calm that followed, the Dragon Mantis showed his face once more. He worked to investigate the fallen, their attires and gear. The sharpness of their blades and the state of their armour. It was quickly found to be lacking and haphazard.

The captured men begged and pleaded for their lives.

Their company lost four apprentices; the assailants lost some thirty men and ten more laid withering in pain like sickly worms.

The Dragon Mantis moved to join Lysiac in interrogation, but the Armsmaster was already impatient and irate.

"These are not rebels." Lysiac fumed at the captured men, pacing before them with his hands in the air. "Rebels move with purpose and stand their ground when tested with steel. The lustre of glittering trinkets and false control does not motivate rebels. They do not cower from their destiny or regret their encounters. What are you? Speak!"

The interrogations were cut short at the realisation that these men were mountain bandits who were rather unwilling to part with any further knowledge than their obvious profession. Whether that was due to lack of said knowledge or some deeper discipline remained a mystery.

The captured men were worked to bury the fallen, then were promptly tied up and pushed forward. The company now choose to forsake any attempt at secrecy, for a band of captured bandits trudged ahead of their force toward the city of Trivagta.

The city of Trivagta was nothing short of impressive. The path leading to it was beset with farmlands stretching as far as the eyes can see, atop hills and across valleys. Tall statues, rather than small straw filled forms, served as scarecrows. Hanging gardens filled with colours could be seen outlining the city as they approached, brim with plants, trees and flowers.

Yet it served little to lighten his mood.

Armsmaster Lysiac remained irritable during the rest of the march, and as soon as they arrived within the city walls, he started barking his commands. He mandated a rally of all captains that had fallen out of favour with their Landmasters. He asked for documents detailing these alleged fallouts. And sent for the Landmasters themselves to justify their actions. Armsmaster Lysiac spoke with much passion and anger that alerted all Trivagta's nobility to note his arrival.

In short, he rattled every Rigatan feather he could.

The Dragon Mantis sent messages ahead and arranged four meetings for the upcoming week.

But the first day passed with nothing noteworthy.

The second proved different.

The company had set up camp, or rather took over, the city's town-hall. Lysiac had his men train in the grounds within, and the Dragon Mantis has his patrol on the grounds without, dressed as townsfolk and beggars.

Of the Rigatans they talked to that day, some were summoned from faraway farmlands or watchtowers, others had a function within the very town-hall the Hydarians had taken over. Yet most of the men they met were rather tame and uncaring, which drew a strange mixture of disgust and anger from Armsmaster Lysiac.

Before midday, as Lysiac escorted one peculiarly thin captain out of the chambers they made into a makeshift interrogation room, accompanied by the Dragon Mantis, a beggar could be heard coughing thrice outside.

"Right this way," Lysiac said as he brought the captain towards the exit.

"I trust everything is in order?" The thin captain asked.

"That remains to be seen." Lysiac spoke, and the Dragon Mantis leaned closer to whisper something quickly into his ear.

"This is all rather-" he paused, "what is *she* doing here?"

"A familiar face?" Lysiac asked.

"One I had told not to follow me here. Excuse me for this, Armsmaster."

"Not at all. Let us go show your friend some courtesy, then."

Lysaic was quick to lead the three of them towards the fair woman, who had an almost restrained, elegant quality about her. As though she were a garden rose left in a field of wild grass.

The Dragon Mantis' eyes darted and saw an entourage was close to the woman. He walked towards the woman and coughed twice, guarding his mouth as he approached.

"Apologies." He spoke in a hoarse tone.

She smiled and offered him a red handkerchief, which he politely refused.

"I thought I had left instruction to remain outside, dove." The captain said.

"Oh, but you were gone for a great length of time. I feared for you." The woman spoke softly.

The captain started walking her out of the building entirely, clearly wanting to get away from the Armsmaster.

And Lysiac followed without a shred of humility.

"You have absolutely nothing to fear for. I am a Rigatan Captain, after all." The slim man said.

"One that is not afforded the luxury of enjoying a simple day." She replied, huffing and giving the Hydarians a side eye.

"Rigatan summers are long, dove, and the day is good still." The slim man grabbed her by the arm now and lead her outside.

"Is it not? The flowers are in a beautiful blossom this summer," the Dragon Mantis started, meticulous in his delivery. "Don't you think so, my lady? I have not seen such alluring shades in all my forty-two years. Nothing would put a damper on this weather, not even if dragons filled the skies."

"Truly," she replied, gazing upwards and shielding her eyes. "Though it has been clouding for the last twenty days now, when it clears, you must see the orchids in full bloom."

"The clouds hide their beauty, do they not?"

The four of them had stopped outside of the interrogation building now. Lysiac's eyes darting between all three around him rapidly. The Rigatan Captain seemed, if nothing else, confused.

"Perhaps that is all there is to these clouds," the woman sighed. "But I am a bard by trade. In our songs, these clouds rise from the smoke of our busy cities, raining down over the mountains and washing into our canals and rivers. That is how I choose to view them."

"An eloquent viewpoint, but I suspect they are merely watering our crops, dove." The captain seemed dismissive of the woman and far keener on moving away from Lysiac.

"Shame, really," the woman continued in response. "Come the end of summer and you'll see what young and ambitious grasshoppers will do to these crops that we so dearly value. Sooner than we all think, I'm afraid, and there is no eloquence to what they bring."

Lysiac continued studying them in silence.

"A shame, truly." The Dragon Mantis replied. "It is an interesting land, this Rigata. The fertility of the land makes the food here to die for, and yet if these pests devour the crops, you are left to starve. Living in luxury, or not at all."

"We look after our common folk in Rigata." The Rigatan captain interjected. "Though I worry more about their survival than their bellies."

"And I do not?" She put her hands to her hips and offered a pout. "I worry about our livelihood. How can we survive without crops and cattle? I worry about every withering flower or caged beast who would rather wander freely through the endless beauty of the west than be made to labour in the fields. Yet without its effort, how would seeds be sown?"

"I am afraid I agree with the esteemed captain." The Dragon Mantis replied. "We have not come to converse as farmers. Excuse us, my lady. It was a delight to meet such an open mind, but I am afraid we have more queries to get to."

"If that is what you call them." The thin captain half snorted as he turned on his heel and gave his escort an expectant gaze, at which she politely bid her farewells and accompanied him.

The two men stood for a while, then exchanged a knowing look. Through what seemed to have been menial chatter, many secrets were exchanged, and many decisions made.

With the streets quiet again, the Dragon Mantis and Armsmaster Lysiac walked back into the safety of the building they had made into a headquarters.

"That pompous fool has let on more than he thought, in vain hopes of scaring me, no doubt." Lysiac announced proudly. "What is happening here is a sham and a mockery of our intelligence. They evict anyone with a remote suspicion of supporting Hydaria or its policies only to feign ignorance. Some even disappear, and their bodies have yet to resurface."

"Far grimmer news than that, I'm afraid." The Dragon Mantis twisted his face in anguish. "The bandits were more than they seemed. They were only meant to disrupt us, but that is not their purpose. They intercepted and destroyed any messages made through our connections. To sever our limbs in the south and leave our spies stranded and desperate, hoping to expose mistakes and have them reveal themselves. They must have intercepted her original reports and destroyed them. We were left with an incomplete picture and so we lacked urgency."

"This was the Orchid Mantis you spoke of then?"

"Yes, but that is not all." The Dragon Mantis paused and looked around. They were now inside a private room, and even then, he inspected every corner and shadow deliberately. "Even more worrying, it appears this was a royal command. And by my reckoning, only few of noble blood reside in these parts, and fewer still can rally the Rigatans behind their banners."

"Rally?!" Lysiac's eyes widened with surprise. "Are we amidst the violent waves of a grand rebellion? Is that what our merry band of some-forty men face? Are you certain of all this information? I assume, gathered through your queer talk with that Orchid?"

"I am unsurprised you've noticed. What else did you make of it?"

At that, Lysiac paused and took to ponder about the exact phrasings of the conversation.

"I am sure. If I have missed no clues, and I do not think I have. They are yet to amass their armies. They're still plucking out traitors and spies, as we can plainly see."

"Truly," Lysiac rubbed his chin now. "Seeing the state of this land, I would assume our luck has yet to fail us. We are early and they have not organised themselves yet. They merely got their orders not a few months past, correct? Strange that the webs untangled so slowly, a credit to our mantises no doubt. We must strike now before they find their footing. Send for our ambassador in the city. He is to use his name and power to arrange for a trial of all the remaining Landmasters and their captains. To be announced as a formality to justify their actions of disposing of all these men that swore allegiance to both our sister nations of Hydaria and Rigata. How to word it? Hm, affable yet firm. We do not wish to override their ruling, but to make sure no injustices found ways to their conclusions. You got that? Make sure to be clear. They will not openly oppose us or insult our ambassador yet, but we wish not to alarm them."

"Are you certain, Armsmaster? You wish us to be trapped in a closed courtroom with our enemies? If we misplace one man or overplay our hand, it will be the end of our company."

"Or the end of theirs." Lysiac smirked now.

"Pride has been the fall of many men."

"Thin lines between pride and flourish, and I require the latter for the bards to sing."

"Is that all that needs be sung then?" The Dragon Mantis asked.

"Almost. I still have more orders."

Lysiac stood over the desk and looked down at notes and reports. Then he smiled to himself.

"Make sure you place a mantis at each of their homes and offices, those accursed elites and highborn. I want to know what they do once summoned to a trial, whose face twists with anger or so much as snorts. I want to know which two decide to meet up in a secret underground room beneath a tavern and how many try to escape the city, or worse, rally its forces. Once inside the courtroom, we will control it and force their hand. Where are our reinforcements? Ah, this is all getting all too interesting."

"On route, but speaking of which, we still have allies within this city, some of which may direly need our help."

DELETERIOUS TIDINGS

FOR THE EYES OF THE SCRYING MANTIS

From the **Foreboding Forest**'s edge, and along the **Silent River**, we have received multiple reports of supernatural events.

Of note is the fact that our intrigue in these misplaced deeds and mis-attributed happenings has ample reason. It came about originally out of increased demands to scout out the area.

Around Yergamond was where our first report originated. A local village chief claimed to have seen an unnatural stream of lightning streak across the sky on a clear night. Though lightning can occur without rain, the man claimed no clouds on that night, and a distinct direction south, towards the forest and along the river.

Following this, we found fishermen claiming to have seen a hill sprout out from one bank of the river. Upon further inspection, the *hill* was only a large mound of dirt, a trick played either upon us by the fishermen or upon them by another. We continued further south.

Nearest to the forest, a butcher claimed to have lost livestock meant for the knife. He mentioned an increased demand for fresh meat to be ready for the army's eventual march. Then claimed strange accounts of a man dressed in white leading cattle into the forest. He sent his own boys to retrieve the cattle, but they never returned.

Our own investigation into the forest was cut short by the need for our eyes elsewhere, but we have already dismissed these reports as dissonance against the war effort. Though the claimants themselves all attributed these happenings to some form of magic.

Skittering Mantis

Flame

12th OF THIRD SUMMER 496 F.O.

The Hydarian ambassador in Rigata, a short balding and otherwise unremarkable looking man, spoke, and no one listened. He stood lazily and strained his voice inaudibly amidst the courthouse centring the Rigatan city of Trivagta. His meek demeanour barely carried the message to the other end of the large round chamber, and murmurs of concern echoed louder than his own words.

"That..." Armsmaster Lysiac snorted, then sighed and turned to lower his tone. "If only in part, explains the audacity of the Rigatans to plan rebellion with no concern for his unwatchful eye. I thought the office of the ambassador commanded order and garnered respect. Respect! Forget that all together. It's a marvel any of our Emperor's orders were ever carried out. This, this embarrassment enforced high taxes and issued a decree for war?"

"That is not the office, Armsmaster." The Dragon Mantis replied sharply. "That is merely its figurehead, one that we must endure during such trying times. Besides, I would tread lightly, Armsmaster. For he is of Hida's Scribes, a bloodline as noble as your own, one dares say. Basis to inspire enough respect as to make up for what otherwise his character finds lacking."

The Armsmaster scoffed, but remained silent.

The day was still fresh and Lysiac had managed little sleep during the past night, and the young Armsmaster yawned and his eyes darted around, then above.

Rigata was a peculiar kingdom, its lush green countryside worked to contrast its marvellous and intricately architected cities. Jewelling the centre of Trivagta were the royal chambers, a tall, layered tower where nobles and highborns reside.

And by its side stood the courtroom.

Lysiac and his company were scattered within the courtroom. He was seated within the lower levels of the many layered courtroom, formed in large concentric steps. These steps doubled as seats for whenever a forum was held there and led down to a small yard. One that was currently occupied with guards clad in deep shades of Rigatan green.

Four gateways led out of the yard, which itself was beset with tiling forming the titular *'Compass of Truth'*, and onto the four exits leading back to the city. Each pointing towards a cardinal direction as mapped out by their Rigatan forefathers.

The ambassador concluded his muffled speech with heaving puffs, mouthed some recognitions for attendance and sighed. He then sped through the otherwise required formal gratitude before sinking back to his chair, like fat congealed to the bottom of a cauldron.

Another man rose and officially started the trial. He was unmistakably Rigatan, with short black hair, a pronounced chin, a wide nose, a large forehead and overall sharp features. His speech was composed and eloquent, evidence of his stature.

Lysiac immediately shifted and sat upright.

"Prince **Gimora**," the Dragon Mantis intervened. "He leads this gathering instead of his absentee brother, Prince Renedil. I understand the Rigatans elected to send one with royal blood as a less than subtle token of apology and a peace offering."

"You understand, or were told?" Lysiac asked.

"I doubted it too, more likely it is a smoke screen, a cheap distraction for our eyes as their agents move in the shadows. It is a surprise he's not introduced himself. I made certain that he was aware of your presence."

"It's merely his second day within the city. We've waited long."

"I do not believe that to be entirely true, his appearance was made public then. Yet, my ears picked up another rumour, one detailing a camp to the north of the city that lasted for three days prior."

"What would he spend three days in the wilderness for?" Lysiac asked.

"I have only speculations."

"The master of knowledge shies from sharing an unfound theory?"

"Securing his entrance, and exit, probably. Plotting the downfall of us proud nosed Hydarians, possibly?"

"You're saying I should be more watchful of my back, are you not?" Lysiac scoffed as he looked at the fierce soldiers standing behind the prince, no doubt his personal guard. "Have you verified all this talk of secret agents? You have! Good, I am quite impressed with your mantises. Honestly, I've grown rather fond of the utility your lot brings. I must always bring your kind along."

"No Battlemaster travels without one."

"Then I must ascend the ranks once more, onto an honoured Battlemaster then."

"Or you can pay my tariff out of pocket." The Dragon Mantis said with a smile, putting his hand on Lysiac's shoulder.

"Quiet now, it's starting."

The trial itself was dimly mundane and pedantic, as if it was made so intentionally by the two residing Rigatan judges alongside the prince and the ambassador. They focused on the very minor details of what had transpired between the captains that had been dismissed and their Landmasters, fixating on the reports written after the fact and whether they had any contradictions with people's retellings.

A cruel demonstration of the tedium of bureaucracy.

Talks were slow and repetitive, and every official would go on for ludicrous lengths of time about the importance of their bookkeeping system. Those that garnered any punishment were those they deemed disorderly, or rather, whose records were. Even then, the punishment came in the form of more rigorous training regimens and oaths to adhere to proper conduct in the future.

The trial dragged on, and managed to entirely ignore, or rather circumnavigate, the Landmasters that had dismissed their subordinates unfairly, albeit allegedly.

Armsmaster Lysiac found his eyes wandering and his mind absent. It took less than an hour before he had completely stopped listening and went back to yawning.

Though others remained vigilant.

Despite the apparent goal of the judges, the Dragon Mantis persevered, his ears pricked, and his eyes tensed. He followed every word and watched their faces like a patient cat stalking a conceited mouse.

For this courtroom was his realm, and in words, he showed his prowess. Armed with a quill and a parchment, he fought his war.

Every pause.

Every change in tone.

Every averted gaze or awkward motion.

He assessed their words, those who spoke too highly of Hydarian sovereignty and those who spoke too aggressively against it. Those who exaggerated their allegiance, and those who cautioned suspicion, he noted them all.

After each short intermission, he would scurry away. Notes were passed to his mantises. Some wore the garb of servants and attendants, others that of guardsmen. He would return with a drink in hand and offer it to Lysiac.

Normal intermissions lasted but a few minutes.

During recess at midday, the Rigatan noble residing over the courtroom stood proudly and clapped his hands thrice. Aides flooded the halls, and a banquet was prepared and served. The attendees and their guards remained in their designated seating arrangements and received their food. Different plates to different folk, as if by rank or virtue.

"Quiet a generous spread." Lysiac said.

His plate was laid in front of by a smiling young woman, and as he politely nodded, his eyes admired his meal. A small fish, some bread and cooked vegetables. He looked at other plates as they passed by and noted meats covered in thick gravy and fragrant wine sauce.

"Though I can forgive favouritism on the best of days, there are traditions that govern treating one's guests, no?" Lysiac asked, but his companion did not reply, his eyes were trailing aides in absolute focus. Lysiac ate in silence as he watched along.

The trial resumed not a full hour after.

To immediate discord.

"They claimed it was treason!" The next man sent to the stands was short, loud, and feisty. "When I had lost a limb to this war of theirs, marching under their command, now *I* am a traitor."

The man's passion awakened the sluggish courtroom, made sleepy by their meal. He pointed his finger directly at the prince and the crowd was in murmurs.

"I am certain that was not the case." One judge interjected quickly, yet he seemed lethargic as he struggled to pick up a parchment and put it against his face. "We have the document from that day here, and it does not mention treason... rather... inability to continue with your tasks. Ah, you're frustrated about-"

"And now I am called a liar," the man erupted. "What else do you wish to pin upon the chest of these delusional fools you call citizens?"

"Settle down, son-" another judge said, then coughed twice. He had both his hands open to calm the soldier, but his arms seized up.

They quickly rushed to loosen his collar as he grabbed at his own throat tightly and began croaking for air.

"Too quickly!" The Dragon Mantis bit his lip and Lysiac sprung to life. "That old judge, he must have had an aliment too strong to withstand it."

The judge coughed again, heaved, and quickly turned pale.

One of the prince's helmeted guards rushed to the judge's side as he collapsed to the ground. Men stood in their seats and guards turned their heads.

The coughing turned to gasps as the guard strained and moved to doff his helmet.

Then it all stopped.

A deliberate moment passed by as the guard put his head against the judge's chest.

"Poisoned!" the guard erupted.

The same guard threw down his helmet, turned to his left sharply and then to face Prince Gimora. The guard then rushed to his ward and promptly planted his fist into the prince's stomach, causing him to throw up his recent lunch.

It all happened in an instant and chaos took the room. Lords and Ladies of Rigata were taken by panic and fear.

Another body collapsed.

The brave of the guards rushed to their lords, and the meek worried for their own bellies.

Men and women were keeling over now, some stood their ground longer and others attempted to push fingers into their own throats. Yet all who survived the poison found short blades planted into their backs before they could recognise friend from foe.

The trap of the mantises was swift and its execution, although staggered, was loosely going in accordance with the Dragon Mantis' plan.

Yet prince Gimora was still alive and reeling. His six guards were now leading him down the monumental steps and to the exit. A few other Rigatan captains and Landmasters saved themselves in time or had not eaten the poisoned food altogether.

"Kill all inside." Came the ominous command from Lysiac.

"Make way." Rigatans ran with weapons in hand now.

"None shall make it to the city. There they will escape us," Lysiac howled as he brandished his weapon. All who had survived the initial onslaught had started a mad dash towards the courtyard. There they noticed that three of the four gates were made to collapse. The fourth, the eastern gate, was barricaded by a few dozen men, now led by Armsmaster Lysiac.

"Move!" screamed the same guard who'd cast away his helmet as he charged at them, and behind all Rigatans followed.

The guard clashed first into Quartermaster Kiganac, and Lysiac felt enough confidence to lead a counter charge for the prince's head.

Lysiac moved gracefully through the small and disorganised courtyard. Holding a longsword with one hand and keeping an array of daggers on his waist and belt.

There was no time to form ranks or follow tactics. The Rigatans pushed to cut through back to the city and the Hydarians wished for a massacre.

Lysiac caught the rampant swinging sword of his first adversary and quickly disposed of the man's head. His aim precise and deadly. He then sidestepped another low strike aimed at his feet, only to turn to the second assailant and launch a dagger at his head. The man swayed to the right and was met with Lysiac's sword ringing against his neck.

Lysiac now faced off with the two remaining helmeted guards separating him from the prince. There, he saw terror between the slits of their helmets.

"Step aside and keep your neck-" Lysiac started, then heard a loud commotion behind him. He turned carefully to not leave his back exposed and found the helmetless guard from earlier lunging at him. Left behind was the lifeless body of his stalwart Quartermaster and many of his young apprentices.

Lysiac clashed with the guard, preparing an insult and a way to put the man to shame before disposing of him. All such thoughts escaped his mind when he was met with the man's deep and fuming green eyes. The guard pushed Lysiac back, and the Armsmaster jumped out of the way, slashing in a circular fashion as to punish any who thought they saw an opening to strike.

The Dragon Mantis alone remained inside the courtroom, and he worked to investigate the fallen bodies before the tense pause promoted him to look to the eastern exit.

Two lines formed now, Lysiac led the Hydarians, clad in different garments of servants, nobles and Rigatan soldiers alike. The other was led by the green-eyed guard, a collection of current and former members of the Rigatan army, and one unarmed prince struggling for his breath and a blade to defend himself.

"You, green eyes. Tell me your name." Lysiac started after a deep breath. "It takes quite the warrior to crush Kiganac. You seem to have done so unscathed."

The guard remained stalwart; his gaze fixated on Lysiac's blade.

"A man of few words, no matter. They say actions speak louder, and you've damn near deafened me."

Lysiac pushed forward again, and the two lines crashed into each other, some crumbled like sand against a high wave, others stood their grounds. It was quickly made evident that their little skirmish held a focal point, and quickly faces turned towards it.

Lysiac's eyes were lit with a demented, eerie glow. In fighting, he found his meaning and against the unyielding foe that remained a nameless guard; he found a queer elation.

They exchanged blows and strikes to no conclusion.

Lysiac fought with intellect and trickery, flinging daggers and cutting at limbs, yet the guard remained steadfast.

They battled until their blades had dulled and splintered by the force of it all. Yet Lysiac could not break his opponent no matter how long they fought. Before long, the city's watch that was already on high alert had caught wind of the events that had transpired within the courthouse.

The Hydarians who stood near the back lines aimed their arrows at those who wished to approach the courtroom. Yet they knew arrows would not dissuade them for too long.

"Armsmaster, we must bar the gates or else we will be swarmed from outside!" The Dragon Mantis' voice called from behind. Lysiac had grown weary and his arms heavy. He lost focus as his head turned and the green-eyed guard slashed at his chest.

The Hydarian Armsmaster fell.

The lines shifted, and the Hydarian apprentices rushed to their Armsmaster. It took a moment of confusion for the Rigatans to cut through the barricade and make their way back to the city.

"We will return," screamed Prince Gimora. "Mark my words, you will live to rue the day that you provoked Rigatan ire. Your storm will come, Lysiac, son of Ragos. You will be taken by the blood and pain of Reyga."

The Dragon Mantis didn't wait for a command. He ordered the collapse of the fourth and last exit before Lysiac had recovered, hoping for the debris to catch the fleeing prince.

'As stubborn as his father, that Lysiac, no matter how much he'd deny it. He would risk all our lives for the honour of killing a nameless, insignificant guard. And here I thought he'd be fighting to avenge his fallen Quartermaster. Look at him, his grin has yet to fade.'

It didn't take long for the city watch to siege the courthouse and try to bring down a wall or two. Yet their progress was painstakingly slow without proper siege equipment. The Hydarians held their position and patiently waited.

One apprentice tended to the Armsmaster's wound, and the bodies were collected and accounted for.

As sunlight faded and night approached. The Dragon Mantis stood by the tall glass windows of the courthouse and observed patiently.

At midnight, he saw a flickering flame atop the northern hills outside the city and a smile drew itself across his lips.

Before dawn, the unwalled city of Trivagta was overrun by the reserves of the second Hydarian army. Any who bore a blade or attempted opposition in any way laid dead in the silent streets of dirt, now drenched in blood.

Morning came and the new arrivals managed to quickly continue the work of the Rigatans. Within hours, they had removed all the blockage from the courthouse's entrance.

Armsmaster Lysiac walked outside to be met by his three Quartermasters.

The muscular and tall **Rtion** was the first to speak, pointing a finger at the Armsmaster's chest, "you were injured?"

"I am quite fine, lively as a sparrow. Ready to sing in joy, once you confirm you've captured the snivelling prince and his company in good health."

"They were long gone before we even arrived, Armsmaster."

Lysiac swore and spat.

"Did you catch their trail?" Lysiac asked after a moment.

"Hardly," Rtion replied slowly, but was quickly interrupted by the Dragon Mantis.

"I expect he's followed whatever plan he prepared for this event. We can safely assume they made for the capital to meet with Prince Renedil."

"Oh," Lysiac said, then turned to face his Quartermasters. "And you've just arrived. Apologise to the men for me, no time to stop for the sights and no rest for the wicked."

The Armsmaster's voice dropped with finality to it.

"We march to lay siege to their capital tonight!"

SAPPHIRE IRE

FOR THE EYES OF THE SCRYING MANTIS
FROM THE BULWARK OF THE SHIELD MANTIS

Grim is the day that a fly would snuff out a mantis, but even in death a mantis leaves behind information.

The camp at **Lake Orta** has been uncovered. The **Sapphire Knight**'s diligent pruning of her own men leaves her free of intrigue and difficult to track. But the lack of recent battle has emboldened her to extend her reach and draw our hand.

The mantises stationed at Lake Orta had been posing as lumbermen and fishermen. A good and convincing role they played out well. The reason they were found out remains unclear to us as of this moment, though their eradication may have been avoidable.

The Sapphire Knight took a small detachment of men and travelled to the mantis camp at Orta. She had arrived with suspicion of mischief, but all accounts claim that she merely thought this new village to be brigands posing as villagers. In either case, we have sent word to every mantis among flies and hornets to redouble their efforts, the **Deadleaf** mantis at the forefront.

She pried into the camp and began asking uncomfortable questions of the mantises, who gravely misplayed their position.

Needless to say, the camp is now no more. The Sapphire Knight is unscathed, and perhaps further made brazen by this victory. Her whereabouts are now known at the very least. She now resides in her namesake city.

Flaming Mantis

Fire

3rd OF FIRST FALL 496 F.O.

In the verdant depths of southern lairs festers a charming **Chanting** Mantis, whose whispers shall now be conveyed concerning the events he bore witness to.

By this point, Armsmaster Lysiac had a complete surround of the Rigatan Capital and was ready to lay waste to their defiance, however, our Chanting Mantis had eyes within the keep to witness a set of happenings important to note, for they motivate future decisions made by the Armsmaster, whose consequences will be felt duly into the future.

***

The throne room in Rigata rivalled anything the minstrel had seen in Hydaria, and he had seen everything.

'Standing here every time, one cannot help but sympathise. They, too, have their noble ancestry.'

The hall was massive.

Fifteen arches held up the elongated dome of the throne room. The very curved ceiling itself was a marvel to behold. Paintings were etched into it, statues were carved from it, and it was made in such a way that the wind would form a pleasant whistle whenever it passed overhead.

Massive verdurous banners hung between the arches, each capturing in gold engravings the insignia of the various noble Rigatan Houses, and atop each banner was a statue of a beautiful bare woman, whose flowing marble hair covered her bosom, and whose midriff was covered by the slack of the banner's top edge.

Fire

The floor was fashioned of a dark sort of marble, and only near the throne were there carpets. The throne itself was a master craft, deep green linings and a golden frame perched atop a step that was covered in a veneer of elegance. To each side of the throne were two full suits of Rigatan armours anchored upon colossal statues. Far behind the throne was an even larger one, signifying the ruling House of Rigata.

It was thereupon that throne Prince Renedil sat, tilted to one side with a pensive expression on his noble face. There sat a man that all of Rigata aspired to become; tall, well built, curled hair that flew like the silver streams that carved the Rigatan countryside. His reputation among the nobility was matched only by the adulation of his people.

And now he faced his darkest hour.

"They have not come!" Prince Averil fumed. "They promise their allegiance, swear that they will do all they can, and in our time of need, they pretend as though the Whistling Court is silent." Prince Averil was standing on the perch of the throne next to his brother's seat.

"Forgive me, Prince Averil, but perhaps the spies we caught had a hand in this treason." The green-eyed guard spoke calmly.

"Truly, such as we intercepted their messages, they must have done ours." Another guard added, a shorter and stockier man with dark skin and trimmed black hair. He stood with both hands clasped behind his back as he addressed their prince apparent.

"I find no amusement in this irony." Renedil said icily, and the guard's head dropped to the ground.

"Farmers, merchants, and craftsmen, were these their claims?" Averil asked.

"Yes, my lord."

"We must assume that the Hydarian web of intrigue runs deeper than just those. How does word reach them of our calls for aid, anyway?"

"Matters little." Renedil sat upright for a moment, and then bent halfway forwards, his arms resting on his thighs as his blank expression trailed across his ancestral throne.

All fell silent.

"Our current predicament is that of a Hydarian upstart with the gall to lay siege to Rigata proper." He continued, his voice unveiling his ire. "I would pick up my sword and honour the memory of every sigil in my father's court, and yet I know I would do so to fall."

"No, brother." Averil shook his head deliberately. "Your safety is imperative for succession. Should you fall, then what little unity we have, even under oppression, will scatter. And you know the Hydarians would love nothing more than seeing us weakened and broken. You know our siblings, and you know me. We are, admittedly, merely patches in your garden. None of us are fit to lead a united Rigata, and even if one of us were fit to do so, the people only answer to you."

"My brother..." Prince Renedil stood and immediately dwarfed Averil as he laid his armoured hands on his shoulders. "If I were to choose, it would have been you. You carry a genuine interest for our people and for what we've inherited. You are wiser than you think you are, and humbler than you claim to be."

"You flatter me, or vastly overestimate me." Averil said.

"I know my brothers; I half raised you and I could not have asked for better siblings. Though allow me to say this, I vow never to force you into that position you fear most."

"Then what are we to do?" Averil asked.

"The Hydarians will forever hold their politics in the highest regard. Then perhaps we shall give it to them." Renedil said.

"This is not something we can talk our way out of."

"I know. Words alone will not carry much weight; offerings are in order."

"Surely Hydaria will not seek more riches than it already has. At least no amount of gold we possess would sway them to turn a blind eye or deter a siege."

"It is not gold that I speak of."

Averil looked around at the two Royal Guards in distress, then back to his brother.

"A siege," Prince Renedil said. "Is it not a simple matter to break one? Truly, one must simply surrender their city."

"My lord?" The green-eyed guard started, but quickly held his tongue.

"We must bide our time here; we are caught unaware and under-prepared. We are to offer an apology, an explanation and a trophy-"

Prince Renedil was keeping his composure as he spoke, yet his voice broke before it could utter the final words. He stood there biting his tongue with a grimace, before turning to shield his face from his own men.

"You do not mean it..." Averil shook his head wearily at the thought.

"They have had their eyes on her for a long while now."

"Sister will never forgive you."

"And even if she did, I will not force her, regardless." Renedil said.

"You know she would fall upon a blade for your vision of Rigata."

Averil started raising his voice as he moved closer.

"Then this is all we can do. She will buy us valuable time, and we will not let her remain in their hands for long."

A grim and grave expression was shared between the two men. They both lamented the cunning of their enemy, and their own haplessness.

"Excuse me, my lord?" The minstrel began, who had been standing by one pillar silently, like a fly on the wall.

Prince Renedil turned with a changed expression and a faint smile. He held a particular fondness for this minstrel, and a peculiar admiration for his wit.

"Go on."

"There may be an alternate solution that does not compromise the princess." The minstrel started.

The princes exchanged a quick look. Averil stood aside, and Renedil walked towards the minstrel, who bowed and started again.

"Surely the Hydarians would be satiated with the head of whomever we tell them began this incursion. He would have to be a loyal man, of unquestionable character and an indomitable heart. Similarly, he would have to be a prominent enough leader for them to believe it, one with the proper agency to manage the whole ordeal."

The wind outside picked up, and what was a normally soothing whistling had changed. It was now made into a melancholic tune as it contrasted the brooding aura made manifest from this suggestion.

"We cannot be thinking of this..." Averil was the one that broke the silence.

"No. We cannot. I will sacrifice none of my retainers for *my* actions." Renedil decided.

"Besides, what if the Hydarians do not trust us? No, brother, remember what Ragos did to our father and uncles. These Hydarians, they are ruthless, they will take your life."

"Is it ridiculously farfetched? Many of our men came to that thinking on their own regard." Renedil challenged now.

"But to suggest they would act on it without our approval?"

"Should we try to convince them one of our Landmasters was to blame, then?"

"My lords." The minstrel interrupted again. "I apologise. These are valid concerns, and yet, there is another concern to be voiced. I believe that the crown prince ought not be in Rigata whenever we open negotiations, regardless of what lure we choose."

"Agreed." Averil added.

"Furthermore," the minstrel said. "I understand the concerns surrounding this next morbid suggestion, but we may not need to deliver them a loyal retainer. We have spies that our Royal Guards captured, correct?"

"What exactly are you suggesting? We barter with spies?" Averil scoffed.

Fire

"No, my lord," the minstrel took out his lute and plucked at it, offering a dark melody befitting the times they lived to see.

"Their plot, we uncovered,
led by the three.
Their treachery, discovered,
as they attempted to flee.

To a warehouse they were chased,
where they raised barricades.
By fire we laid waste,
to their incursion of blades.
Charred corpses we offer,
nothing but burnt lies.
For these bodies had no honour,
return to them their spies."

Averil frowned, but Renedil visibly grimaced. He understood exactly what his minstrel was insinuating through his brief song.

"That is a tall tale, and one that stands on shaky feet." Averil said. "I cannot say with confidence that it will be believed."

"It will be enough," Renedil said. "For it will come with all that I've offered, an apology and a trophy. I've said it before and I will say it again. This Lysiac is an upstart. He will be sated with the lowered head of a royal and the hand of another. It ought to be enough to shape his legacy, let him return to his north and wallow in his vain pride."

"This is a gambit, brother."

"Do you trust yourself to it, Averil?"

"For Rigata green." Averil saluted with an unsure smile.

"Bring me the spies you caught." Prince Renedil's voice was low and gravelled as he ordered his guards. "And ready your finest men. They are to escort me out of the city as best you know how."

"At once," the green-eyed guard responded promptly. "The irrigation system passes below the city in tunnels and would be well hidden from prying eyes, my liege. I know men who would gladly guide us through it and underneath the siege."

"Then that will be our path. What of the spies?" Renedil asked.

"They are held in the dungeons; I shall go fetch them and ready myself for the extraction."

"No. You are to remain here with my brother." Renedil decided, making the guard's brows raise in shock. "I shall be safe, and I shall muster an army the likes of which Hydaria could only dream of."

Renedil turned to visible confusion.

"I said we must stall for time, but it shan't be long. This Hydarian army will not return past our borders. The time to strike is now. If these are the extremes we are led to, then the iron has never been hotter. When we burn the spies and present them as our Landmasters in an effort to delay our enemies, then truly, we must not delay any further."

"What am I to do?" Averil asked.

"Delay them here, brother. For I aim to pincer them near Trivagta. I will aim to return within two weeks. Open the gates and negotiate, slowly, and when negotiations conclude, prepare a banquet."

Averil stood stunned as he wrapped his mind around the plot that was unravelling before him.

The minstrel simply bowed, and the guards made their way to the cells to bring the spies. The stockier guard would then escort these spies to a warehouse that he would make the necessary arrangements, to have it be burnt down with the men trapped inside.

The green-eyed guard arranged for the company to escort Renedil out of the city, of tried and trusted men without a blemish on their records. Then he returned to the Whistling Court.

There, Averil remained in a daze as the world moved around him while he stood motionless, peering from a widow as a fire began in his city. A fire that he knew the cause of.

Fire

The Rigatan prince remained in a state of paralysis during the next day, as the Landmaster in charge of the capital's defence received the news. Days passed, yet he remained motionless as the siege was broken and negotiations started. Even as cruel sabatons of the Hydarian Armsmaster clinked triumphantly onto the marble floor of their ancient court, Averil stood.

But there was also the sound of chains.

"Prince Averil!" Lysiac began emphatically, and the green-eyed guard wrapped his hand around his sword in anticipation. "It is good that we finally get to speak, wouldn't you agree? For it was a true shame I never managed a conversation with your younger sibling, Prince Gimora."

The city had been surrendered, Renedil had escaped, and the charred corpses of the spies that had been fitted with Rigatan armaments were presented to Lysiac as the traitors.

Their hand had been played.

Averil thought he could still see the warehouse fire from the window as he turned to face Lysiac. Without a response, he turned. Yet his face twisted as he saw the many men Lysiac had walked into the courtroom, bound in chains together by the neck and hands.

"Who... are these men?" Averil asked.

"You tell me." Lysiac replied in a low tone, then casually shrugged. "Spies, traitors, messengers asking for aid? Who knows, really? I take it the insurrectionists have been dealt with?"

"It has been taken care of, my lord." Averil bit his tongue as he watched the vacant expressions of the chained men.

"And where is your crowned prince? Where is the man Rigata speaks of so highly, Prince Renedil?"

"He is abroad, my lord. Negotiations with Vera have been taking up his attention of late." Averil struggled, and the guards tensed. "Yet he would have also approved of the burning of traitors. There is no place for mistrust amongst allies, lest doubt seep in the minds of lesser men."

Averil held himself high, and spoke with royal eloquence, yet the response from the Hydarian 'upstart' deflated his proud chest once more.

"That's good." Lysiac spoke in a manner that flourished confidence. "I must say, you Rigatans are ruthless with your traitors. As allies, we must be united in our response to treason as well as our fight against it, correct?"

Lysiac took out his sword, brandished it around and at a single command, the messengers were brought to their knees.

"Armsmaster Lysiac, surely there is no reason to sully this ancient court in-"

A corpse collapsed.

Averil's words fell on Lysiac's deaf blade as he methodically beheaded the first of the messengers. Then moved slowly to another, painting the marble floor of the Whistling Court in deep blood red as he did.

"What do you say? Let us begin anew?" Lysiac offered as he cleaned his blade between beheadings. Forcing the frightened men to exude worried sounds and pleading motions towards their prince to save them.

The Rigatan guards tensed, yet Averil's gaze remained vacant.

"Prince Averil, imagine what we can accomplish when we truly band together. It is these consistent interruptions that allow Migora to remain sovereign. Not to mention Motra to keep its mountain, and Vera to find new foolish ways to rule without a king."

"A grave misunderstanding and incompetence on our part, Armsmaster." Averil said, grinding the words out from between his clenched teeth.

"We have a mutual understanding then."

"Yes, Armsmaster, we shall weed out any more insurgents, as ever we tried. No price is too expensive for peace." Averil said.

"Splendid, nothing would warm my heart more." Lysiac opened his arms now.

"A cause for celebration then, a banquet is in order!"

"A wonderful thought, truly. Let the red of wine replace the red of blood, do you not agree?"

"Yes, Armsmaster Lysiac."

The court was cleaned, and the rest of the messengers were spared. Preparations were underway for the upcoming banquet in honour of their renewed alliance and the Hydarian Armsmaster. All proceedings were done slowly, under the direct command of Rigatan Royal Guards, yet their royal prince remained distracted.

Averil spent the rest of those days standing by the window watching imaginary flames flicker at a fire, long since doused. His eyes did not move from the warehouse.

And all they would see was fire.

SLUMBERING GIANT

FOR THE EYES OF THE SCRYING MANTIS

Far in the south, beyond the realms of **Motra** and Rigata, lies the once mighty, ever fractured, Archony of **Vera**. Though if reports are to be believed, then it might find salvation in the twin fools of all its rulers.

It is said that the two Archons of the violet realm have met in secret. The Archons of **Verga** and **Voraga** seek to reunite their lineage's heritage. Though it is the reason that is startling. Our mantises themselves claim that the two Archons of the south truly believe that they fight giants. Physical giants of a village named **Vara**. It is out of a blatant inability at defeating these *giants* that the two Archons seek unison, and seek to fill the vacant role of Great Archon.

This Vara, however, is so well veiled by the spikes that decorate the southern edge of the world that our mantises have found great difficulty in ever reaching it. We therefore conclude that our network in the south is not as strong as it once was.

We have sent a few to bolster our ranks in fractured Vera. We will continue to keep a vigil over this region, lest we find a resurgent nation, even if it resides in the far southern twilight of the land.

Meticulous Mantis

Ash

16th OF FIRST FALL 496 F.O.

What now follows is once more a reconstruction of Armsmaster Lysiac's telling of events. At this juncture, many important decisions were made, and some of which were not documented in full official reports. Armsmaster Lysiac was more than courteous to provide his full account, even of undocumented events. His loyalty to Hydaria remains unquestionable, and his commitment indefatigable.

***

Three oversized tables were laid out in the massive dining hall in the ancient palace of Rigata. One table spanned nearly the width of the entire hall, then two more beyond the first were a third of its size and were neatly aligned with the first.

Two sprawling carpets were laid out, green, gold and blueish black were the colours of choice for the elegant-looking floor ornaments.

Between the two smaller tables were some stone stairs that led up to a high table, upon which Lysiac sat alongside Prince Averil. With the green-eyed guard looming nearby, and elsewhere in the corner of the room, the minstrel played a happier tune.

More prominently, however, was the sole woman that shared their table. Princess **Layra**, whose beauty was not exaggerated in the slightest. Her skin was of a darker hue than the noble ladies of the north, and her beauty was a fuller one. Her brows were untrimmed, her cheeks unblushed, her lips were full, and she radiated an unpowdered natural beauty to behold.

And around the Hydarian Armsmaster, she was deathly silent.

"Your forefathers were incredible builders, Prince Averil." Lysaic offered plainly as he twirled a goblet of wine.

"As were yours, Orvabad is another bigger marvel to behold." Averil replied courteously.

"When did you last visit my home city?"

"I was a child still; years have passed since then."

"Still, the sight of the Blood Keep never escapes one's mind." Lysiac boasted, and Averil smiled and raised his goblet.

Lysiac took another sip that trickled red across his lips before looking down at their table.

'Playing at royalty will forever be the fate of the Rigatans.'

He watched the intricate goblets, the laid-out silver chalices, the many candelabras presented all over the table. The bowls of fruit laid out lavishly, the excessive plates and platters of stuffed pork, roasted chicken, and sliced beef lathed in a veneer of mouth wetting garnishes.

'Though this is a true display of overcompensating in generosity, one must enter with an army to be treated as a guest, it seems.'

"Tell me, it has been more than a week now since this *issue* was squashed." Lysiac began as he set down his goblet and leaned back in his highchair comfortably.

"Feels as though a season has passed, no?" Prince Averil tried, but Lysiac did not humour him with a response.

"Where *is* Prince Renedil?" Lysiac asked, "I wish to see him before my days here are done. You know I am to return to Orvabad immediately, but I cannot fathom leaving without congratulating Prince Renedil on his bright sibling that might have just saved his realm."

"I have sent messengers, Armsmaster." Prince Averil started cautiously. "They will report back soon, I hope."

'He isn't even lying, for we intercepted some of them. Oh, I know how you loath me so, poor princeling. And oh, how I am certain that you wish to be rid of me, but I insist.'

"Such a shame." Lysiac shook his head, then abruptly stood up. "Well, there is nothing to it."

"You are to leave?" Averil hid his joy well.

"Promptly, though, before I leave, I must commend you. You've handled this all with such grace, befitting a proper Rigatan prince."

"For Rigata Green." Averil repeated.

"See, I believe you are a good man, Prince Averil. You have only your realm's best interest at heart, so I will leave you with one last gift."

"Surely, gifts are unnecessary, Armsmaster Lysiac." Averil too stood up and began to sweat profusely.

"Oh, but I insist." Lysiac said.

"Gifts ought to be exchanged, and I am afraid we have nothing arranged for this occasion-"

"Nonsense. I am certain we can arrange something." Lysiac smirked and let out a loud, practised whistle.

"Armsmaster Lysiac?"

No sooner had the whistle echoed in the large hall than a detachment of Hydarian soldiers marched pompously into the hall.

With them they dragged a chained and covered up figure.

"Lords and ladies of Rigata." Lysiac hopped to the top of the table and extended his arms. Meanwhile, the Royal Guard instinctively pulled Prince Averil to one side and the minstrel's merry tune simply died down. "I applaud you for taking care of your traitors with such impunity! But I am afraid that my tireless eyes have reported a puppeteer that you were all unaware of."

"Armsmaster Lysiac! We have already dealt with the threat. There is no puppeteer." Averil insisted, but Lysiac ignored him. He leapt off the table and walked to the figure that had been brought to the middle of the hall.

More Hydarian soldiers streamed into the tense hall as even the murmurous cloud of whispers that had hung about had been lifted. The Rigatan guards within the hall were quickly surrounded and outnumbered, though no blades were drawn. The standoff had begun and exchanged looks of panic ran rampant once more. A detachment of Hydarian archers was the last to make its way inside, along with a tall Hydarian Quartermaster who walked closer to the covered figure.

"I assure you, the reports I received are true." Lysiac's voice was almost theatrical as he grabbed the bag that covered the figure before him. "And I assure you, that from this day forth, no more dissent will ever live on in Rigata. It shall be eradicated."

"None does, there is no dissent other than whatever your reports fashioned in fiction!" Averil pushed past the guard and walked closer to Lysiac, and still he was ignored.

"Time and time again have your people heard lies about us northern folk, about the yoke of Hydarian rule. I am here today to unveil the mouth of these lies, the snake in your garden, and the instigator of all your hardships. Consider this my last gift to you, to all of you."

The only man that stood next to the Armsmaster was his muscular Quartermaster Rtion.

"And let this be an exchange of gifts, both of equal value." Lysiac's hand clenched around the bag, ready to lift it off. "In return for cleansing your realm of dissidents, I ask that a piece of your realm travel back north to Orvabad with me. I ask for the hand of Princess Layra in marriage."

"That is absurd-"

Lysiac pulled off the bag and Averil froze once more, this time in shock. He stared and blinked, yet his eyes refused to change the image, and he wept as he saw the bruised and beaten noble face of his brother, the crown prince himself.

Renedil was on his knees, gagged, bleeding and bruised, and looked to be heaving in pained breaths.

"Behold, the traitor!" Lysaic yelled, but the hall would not be stunned for much longer.

Lords took to their feet spewing insults, ladies heckled, the Rigatan guardsmen in the room pulled out their weapons, and the

Hydarians brandished theirs in return. The Royal Guard had already unsheathed his own sword and looked for every angle of approach to attack Lysiac.

"Let this be such a day that will be remembered in Rigata for as long as your kingdom survives. For it is the day Rigata gave up any hope of rebellion." Lysiac yelled again as he, too, took out his blade and pulled back Renedil's head by his long-ruffled hair.

"Lysiac do not dare! Anything but-" Averil found his tongue and screamed, but chaos had already erupted.

Blades clashed against one another, ringing as though they were clappers tolling the bowls of their bells as they fought. However, as with any military encounter where one side is completely unprepared, the results were expected and were achieved with frightening quickness.

Weapons were dropped, and bodies were restrained against the marble floor. Many resisted and none surrendered, but to no avail.

The Hydarian contingents had complete control over the situation. Only the green-eyed guard's blade was left clashing against Rtion's.

In all his years, Rtion swore he had never suffered a more determined and ferocious assault than the one he saw from the Rigatan guard that day. Their engagement only lasted for a moment and it involved three violent offensive moves from the guard, which Rtion barely blocked. The sequence ended with the big muscular Hydarian being thrown across the room. His foe having tripped him in the same opening flurry, then shoved him with a mighty swing.

The guard quickly turned to set his sights on Lysiac, but instantly his eyes widened, and his heart sank. His hands shivered as he beheld Prince Renedil's head fly off his torso and fall by his own feet.

The guard was likened by all who witnessed him to a wild cornered beast, right until he saw his master's headless body. All sense and wit were drained from his body at this instance.

"You will all live and die under Hydarian rule. The sooner you accept it, the sooner tragedies cease within your ranks," Lysiac said.

The Hydarian Armsmaster spat as he wiped his blade clean again and walked towards the princess to further add insult to injury.

"Now I shall collect my reward, and I promise, you shall never see my face in this corner of Osgara again."

The restrained guards struggled, the weaponless lords picked at their cutlery, and their servants stared in horror.

The green-eyed guard's grip around his sword's hilt nearly broke it that day. He readied himself to attack Lysiac, resigned to death but compelled to at least exact vengeance on the arrogant Armsmaster.

"Stand down. Everyone, stand down!"

This was not the voice of Averil. He was on the ground, shaking. This was not Lysiac's voice, nor was it any lord present. This was the princess, taking to her feet, and realising that the archers were now trained upon her brother and his guard, ready to fire.

"There is nothing to fight for here." She pulled her skirt along as she left the dining table and was met by Lysiac at the steps. "If I am bound to Orvabad, then I will leave of my own accord. Not in chains like some prize, is that clear, Armsmaster?"

The princess' voice was laced with poison, full of fury, teeming with hatred, and yet it came out even more composed than Lysaic's in that situation.

"I would have it no other way, my lady." Lysiac said.

Layra wanted nothing more than to reward his smirk with spit, but she collected herself, and left the hall. She did not for one moment look at her brother's severed head, for she could not bear to see it. Rtion, who had recovered to his feet, took a group of men and followed the princess. Meanwhile, Lysiac saw what had become of Averil, still in shock on the ground, and decided that this experience would be enough of a lesson for the Rigatans.

"Prince Averil, I am certain that your rule will be more peaceful. But know this. If I am sent south again, then I will not be as merciful as I am now."

With that, Lysiac left Averil whimpering and the fierce guard's ever green eyes without their colour. The guard did not remain on his knees for long, as he went to collect the still bleeding head of his former prince.

Armsmaster Lysiac had excelled at his task. He had done everything that was expected of him and more. It was at the very tail end of his reports that he mentioned seeing the Rigatans gathered around a field of evergreen grass. More men kneeling than standing.

This was how he left Rigata.

To reports of a burning body, the body of Prince Renedil, no doubt.

And his ashes were duly scattered.

www.ingramcontent.com/pod-product-compliance
Lightning Source LLC
LaVergne TN
LVHW041438170726
843492LV00008B/2669